A Day in the Life of Angelica

by David Lewman

Scholastic Inc.

New York Toronto London Auckland Sydney
Mexico City New Delhi Hong Kong

Table of Contents

Hello! This is going to be your most special day ever. Know why? 'Cause you get to spend it with me—Angelica, the most prettiest, beautifullest, smartest girl in the world! You are SO lucky!

A Is for Angelica!

I'd like to start the day with a nice cheer.
(Remember, you're s'posed to cheer
REALLY LOUD.)

A is for AWESOME, which is what I am!
N is for NICE as a sweet little lamb
G is for the GREATEST girl you ever met
E is for EXCELLENT (and I am, you bet!)
L is for LOVELY, which is what my eyes are
I is for I'M gonna be a great big star!
C is for CYNTHIA, my bestest friend! And . . .
A is still for AWESOME—

YELL IT AGAIN!
ANGELICA! ANGELICA!
GOOOOOO, ANGELICA!
YAAAAAAAAAY!

Lookin' Good

Let's see, what shall I wear today? My daddy says I look like an angel no matter what I put on . . . and you know what? He's right! See, I look good in my . . .

• cheerleader clothes (The "V" stands for "Very Best Cheerleader in the World.")

• detective clothes (You can call me "Shirlylock Holmes.")

• skating clothes

• new Dummi Bears T-shirt

• hiking clothes

• grown-up lady clothes

• or my purple jumper, orange shirt, polka-dot tights, orange socks, and purple shoes!

Now I look beautiful! (Even more than before.)

My Beautiful Hair

After I get dressed, I get my hair put in pigtails. No, that does NOT mean I'm a pig! Who said that? Whoever said that is in pig trouble! I mean BIG trouble!

I have blond hair just like my mommy. No, not POND hair— blond hair!

When my hair is wet, I'm still beautiful, but I'm beautifuller when my hair gets dried. My mommy blows hot air on it with the hair fryer.

Then she puts my hair in pigtails. She brushes my hair into two parts, and then puts a purple ribbon around each pigtail.

My mommy wears her hair in a ponytail. No, that does not mean my mommy is a pony. But someday she's going to buy me one.

There! All done! Gee, my mommy made my hair perfect AGAIN. How does she do it?

How to Be a Princess

My daddy calls me lots of names besides Angelica—Pumpkin, Cupcake, Peanut Nose—but the name I like best is "Princess." It's fun being a princess. You can be one too! (Boys have to be princes.) Here's how:

- call your daddy and mommy "the king and queen"

- sit on a throne (the potty doesn't count)

- wear a crown instead of a hat (you can get one at Burger Doodle)
- move into a big castle
- stay asleep until a handsome prince kisses you (If the prince is ugly, keep snoring.)
- get your friends to bow whenever you walk into the room
- say, "Look at my daddy and mommy!" when you see the king and queen in a deck of cards
- stick a pea under your mattress. Then pull it out and say, "So THIS is what's been keeping me awake."
- stay away from frogs, or you might have to kiss them

Mommy's the Boss

My mommy goes to work just about every day. She's very important, that's why she's the boss. I'm not sure what she does all day, but I think she . . .

- gets foxes from people through the fox machine
- makes some kinda dessert called "takeovers"
- goes to meetings where everyone's bored. They're called "bored meetings."
- talks to Jonathan a lot. He must not be able to hear very well, because she always has to yell.
- sits behind the biggest desk in the world
- looks out the big windows
- buys stuff over the phone, like companies

- rides up and down on the elevators
- fires anyone who says her daughter isn't beautiful
- thinks about what to buy me on her way home!

And I KNOW everyone at work has to do everything she says, 'cause she's the boss!

If I Were the Boss

Someday I wanna be a boss
just like my mommy.
I know JUST what I'm
gonna do when I'm boss!
Let me tell you, I'll . . .

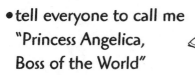

- tell everyone to call me
  "Princess Angelica,
  Boss of the World"
- wear a beautiful suit
- work at a desk that's bigger than a car
- take lots of cookie breaks
- be the only one who wears pigtails
- paint polka dots on the office walls in my
  favorite color
- hire Tommy, Chuckie, Phil, and Lil, so I can tell
  them what to do all day
  (I've had lots of practice!)

- let Cynthia answer my phone
- have big scary robots to chase anyone who doesn't do what I say
- make everyone play tag (but I'm NEVER "It")
- let Fluffy play in my office
- get lotsa free toys and candy
- keep all the money for myself!

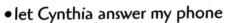

Can you tell I'm gonna be the bestest boss there ever was?

Big Kid Stuff

Because I'm a big kid, I can do lots of things the stupid babies can't do. You're a big kid too, aren't you? Yeah, I thought so. We big kids can do a lot of stuff today. We can

- be on a soccer team (I like the kicking part the best.)

- stay up as late as we want (until Daddy finds us)

- play with lipstick

- eat chocolate ice cream for breakfast

- drink out of sippy cups, instead of baby bottles

- dribble—a basketball, I mean

- watch a movie only us big kids can understand, like *Reptar Meets the Dummi Bears*

- send Chuckie into outside space

- use scissors

- sing in a choir

•use tape

•catch butterflies

•and read a scary book!

21

Mine, Mine, All Mine!

I wonder what we should play with today. There are plenty of toys to play with. You can play with anything that's yours. But here's what's mine:

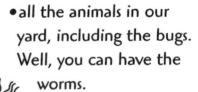

- all the crayons, except the broken ones. Um, the broken ones are mine too.
- everything in my room
- all the plants in our yard
- all the animals in our yard, including the bugs. Well, you can have the worms.
- all of Cynthia's things, including her sports car, her snowmobile, her X-ray machine, her jasusy, her parachute, and her submarine

- anything that flies over our yard
- all the clouds in the sky
- the Statue of Slipperdy
- the Graham Canyon
- the moon
- the sun

- everything that starts with A, including a doll, a toy, a book. . . . You get the idea!

My Friend Fluffy

One of the bestest things that's mine is my cat, Fluffy. She's very nice. (You can pet her if you want. Oh, don't worry about her claws. She's just playing.) I do lots of nice things for Fluffy, like . . .

- put bows in her hair
- let her eat all my broccoli
- drop cookie crumbs all over the house so mice will come inside. Fluffy loves to play with mice!
- let her drink milk—unless it's chocolate
- let her pounce on things that move, so I wiggle Daddy's tie for her
- let her take my nap for me
- and just before she knocks something over with her tail, I knock it over so she won't get in trouble

I love you, Fluffy! Fluffy? Fluffy, come back here!

Taking Care of Grown-ups

Taking care of grown-ups is almost as hard as taking care of cats. But here's what to do if you want nice, friendly grown-ups that do ezzackly what you tell 'em to do:

- Be patient. When it comes to learning stuff, grown-ups are kinda slow. You'll probably have to teach them over and over and over until they get things right.
- Feed them whatever's in the 'fridgergator.
- Walk them around the park.

- Act real nice around them. Smile. Talk in a little, high voice. And close your eyes and open them real fast a buncha times in a row. They like that a lot.
- Hide their stuff. Then find it and ask for a reward.
- If Mommy says no, ask Daddy.
- If Daddy says no, ask Mommy.
- Ask them for stuff when they're sleepy. First thing in the morning is good.
- If you really, really want something, and they're wide awake, wait till they're in a big hurry. Just before they go out the door is good.
- If you see another grown-up doing something good, like giving a kid a toy, be sure to point it out to your grown-ups. Say, "Look, there's a very GOOD grown-up!"
- Every once in a while, give them a little treat, like one of your drawings.
- When in doubt, cry (LOUD!).

Oh, by the way, this stuff works for me. But be careful. One time this kid tried some of my tricks, I mean tips, and he got in BIG trouble. Good luck!

Super Cynthia!

Cynthia is the bestest doll in the whole mooniverse. Why do I say she's the bestest? BECAUSE I DO, THAT'S WHY! Here's what makes Cynthia so great:

- When I ask her to do something, she never says no.
- Her hair's easy to cut.
- Her name ends with an "a," just like mine.
- When we sing together, I can always hear myself.

- Cynthia always needs more things, which means MORE PRESENTS!

- You can bury her in the dirt or send her down the potty, and she'll be okay. Trust me, I know.

- If her head pops off, Daddy can put it back on again.
- Spike can chew on her, or a fish can swallow her, and she'll STILL be okay.
- She's easy to hide so I don't have to share her.
- She likes being a princess, just like me.

Okay, now you can play with Cynthia. Hmm, that's funny . . . I can't find her. Oh, well, that's too bad. I guess you'll have to play with another doll. (Heh, heh, heh!)

Angelica's Lessons

Let's play school! Of course, I'll be the teacher. We'll start by singing the natural anthem, "Angelica, the Beautiful." Now here's what you need to know about . . .

Dance:
Who's the bestest dancer ever?
Me!

Rithmatricks:
If you asked me for two cookies, three cupcakes, and five Reptar bars, how many treats would you have?
None, cause I wouldn't give you any! I'd eat them all myself! Ha!

Geograffiti:
If Tommy took my hat and jumped into the biggest ocean in the world, what would he be in?
Big trouble for getting my hat wet!

'Splorers:
What did Chuckie discover at the North Pole?
That he was scared and wanted to go home!

Music:
Who's the bestest singer ever?
Me!

Science:
Which vegetables are the prettiest?
Pickles, of course!

History:
Which day is the most important day in the
history of the world?
The day I was born!

Art:
What do
you get
when Phil
and Lil paint?
A big mess!

History, again:
Who's the bestest teacher in history?
You guessed it—ME! YAAAAAY, ANGELICA!

Class dismissed.

Snacktime

All this teaching is making me hungry. Luckily, I hid some healthy snacks right here in my room!

Let's have some cookies. The crunching is good for our teeth.

And jelly beans. Everybody knows beans are good for you.

And brownies. It's important to eat a square meal.

And ice cream. To keep cool so we don't get a temperature.

And Reptar Bars. To grow big and strong, like Reptar!

And cupcakes. Anything that comes in a cup is good for you.

And fudge. Chock-full of fudgy goodness.

And pudding. It, uh, tastes good.

And finally, Dummi Bears. They're sticky, so they clean all the other food off our teeths.

Oooh, I don't feel so good now.

Sing Along with Angelica

Maybe we'll feel better if we sing. I'll teach you the words to some songs I know, and then we can sing them together. 'Course you don't sing as PRETTY as I do, but we'll have fun anyway.

Mine, Mine, Mine, All Mine
(to the tune of "Row, Row, Row Your Boat")

Mine, mine, mine, all mine,
Everything is mine!
Share with me, share with me,
Share with me, share with me,
Or I'll start to whine.

If You Think That I Am Pretty

(to the tune of "If You're Happy and You Know It")

If you think that I am pretty, clap your hands.
If you think that I am pretty, clap your hands.
If you DON'T think I am pretty, you'll get
  bitten by my kitty.
If you think that I am pretty, clap your hands.

If you really like my singing, stomp your feet.
If you really like my singing, stomp your feet.
If you DO NOT like my singing, then your ears
  will soon be stinging.
If you really like my singing, stomp your feet.

Cousin Tommy's Little Dog
(to the tune of "Twinkle, Twinkle, Little Star")

Cousin Tommy's little dog,
You are ugly as a frog.
Dogs are yucky,
Dogs are dumb.
Dogs will slobber on your thumb.
Cousin Tommy's little dog,
You are smelly as a hog.

Angelica Is a Big Genius

(to the tune of "My Bonnie Lies Over the Ocean")

Angelica is a big genius.
Angelica is really smart.
Angelica is a big genius.
Her IQ goes right off the chart.

She is
So smart—
She's smarter than anyone else we know.
She is
So smart—
I think I can see her brain grow.

What Are Babies Good For?

Just when we was having fun singing, those dumb babies show up and ruin everything. Tommy, Chuckie, Phil, and Lil are nothing but trouble.

On second thought, there are a FEW things babies are good for, like . . .

- hiding spills (just pick up a baby and plop it down on the spill)
- wiping up spills (those diapers are made to hold puddles)
- taking the blame for broken stuff (you can say they did it; the babies can't say anything)
- taking the blame for stinky smells
- cleaning your hands (just wipe them on the baby's hair)
- dancing in your ballet (mine was called "Angelica's Lake")
- being the brides and brooms in pretend weddings
- working for me in my pretend company
- being your "show-and-tell" at school (I took Tommy)

- getting you cookies and candy (just tell 'em it's for kidnappers)
- working at your lemonade stand (but don't share the dimes)
- being in your circus or your freak show
- being in your Thanksgiving Day parade

But the bestest thing dumb little babies are good for is letting everyone see how smart and grown-up YOU are!

Daddy's Home!

Daddy, Daddy, Daddy!

Big hug, Daddy!

Daddy, what did you bring me?

Fix this toy, Daddy!

Look at Cynthia's new hairdo!

I'll pull your tie off for you, Daddy!

Come see what I drawed today!

When are you going to buy me Outer Space Cynthia?

I'll help you pick out a TV channel, Daddy!

Look at me, Daddy!

Today I played with my new friend, Daddy!

Can I try on your glasses, Daddy?

41

I'm Spoiled—NOT!

Some people say my daddy and mommy spoil me, but they are WRONG! I know what spoiled means. You're spoiled if . . .

- at night your daddy wears a beeper so you can beep him for drinks of water

- after your birthday the toy store has to close down until more toys come in

- everyone who works at your town's amusement park knows your name

- your daddy and mommy get rid of their furniture to make room for your stuff

- if vegetables accidentally get on your plate, your mommy gets you a clean one

- you tell your mommy and daddy when it's time for THEM to go to bed

- the only chore you do around the house is taste-test the desserts

- if you draw on the walls, your mommy and daddy put blue ribbons on your drawings

HEY! WAIT A MINUTE—this sounds like me!
Um, forget I said anything. "Spoiled" is a really
dumb word.

Angelica's Bedtime Story

My daddy always tells me a story before I fall asleep. Here's the bestest story he ever told (the way I remember it).

Once upon a time there was a beautiful little girl named Cindergelica. She was a princess, but nobody knew it.

"Oh, Fluffy," she said to her beautiful white cat, "why doesn't anyone know that I'm really a princess?"

"Meow," said Fluffy.

"What kind of a stupid reason is that?" asked Cindergelica.

All of a sudden— *POOF!*—a puff of smoke came up out of the floor! Then a very pretty lady (but not as pretty as Cindergelica) stepped out of the smoke.

"(Cough, cough!) Hello," said the lady. "I am Cynthia, your fairy dollmother."

"Well it's about time you showed up," said

Cindergelica, putting down her broom.

"I was busy shopping for this sparkly dress," said Cynthia. "Do you like it?"

"Yeah, it's all right," answered Cindergelica. "Listen, Fairy Dollmother, nobody knows that I'm a princess, and it's really starting to bug me."

"All you have to do is go to the Royal Ball tonight and dance with the prince," Cynthia said. "Then he'll marry you and tell everyone you're a princess."

"That's a good plan, Cynthia," said Cindergelica, "but what am I going to wear? And how will I get there?"

Then Cynthia took the wand out of her Fairy Dollmother Cynthia kit and waved it at Cindergelica. *POOF!* Her outfit turned into a beautiful polka-dotted dress and glass hair bows.

POOF! Fluffy turned into a red sports car. *POOF!* Cindergelica's broom turned into a matching polka-dot purse. Inside were the keys to the sports car.

"Wow!" said Cindergelica. "Can you turn Tommy, Chuckie, Phil, and Lil into bugs?"

"No," said Cynthia, "they're already at the ball."

"Thanks, Fairy Dollmother!" said Cindergelica, jumping into the car. "Don't wait up for me!"

"Okay, but remember, you have to be back here by your bedtime—8:30 sharp."

"Aw, can't I stay up an extra hour?" whined Cindergelica.

"NO!" said Cynthia. "Fluffy doesn't LIKE being a car, and she'll need to change back."

Cindergelica was the most beautiful girl at the ball—much more beautiful than Lil. Tommy, Chuckie, Phil, and Lil all asked Angelica to dance, but she danced every dance with a very handsome prince. The prince wanted to marry her. But at 8:30 she had to run away.

Uh-oh, thought Cindergelica, I forgot to tell the prince my name. I'd better leave him a little something.

So she took one of the glass bows out of her hair and tossed it down on the stairs.

But it broke.

"Oh, brother," said Cindergelica. She ran to her sports car, and just before it turned back into Fluffy, she called her fairy dollmother on the cell phone.

"Look," she said, "I didn't get to tell the prince my name, so I really need to stay up an hour past my bedtime. Pretty please with sugar on top?"

"Okay," said Cynthia, "just this once."

Cindergelica ran back into the palace and told the prince her name, address, and phone number. Then her car turned back into Fluffy, so she had to walk home. But the next day the prince came and married her. And then he told everyone she was a real princess. The end.

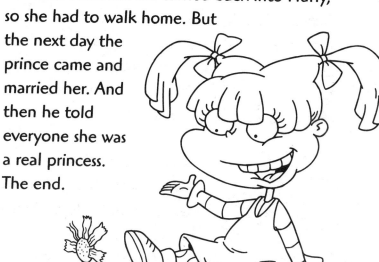